This book belongs to:

L U C A S

D0560558

Published by Ladybird Books Ltd
80 Strand London WC2R 0RL
A Penguin Company

15 17 19 20 18 16 14

© LADYBIRD BOOKS LTD MCMXCVIII

Printed in Italy

Peter and the Wolf

illustrated by Richard Hook

Once upon a time, Peter and his grandfather lived in a house next to a beautiful green meadow.

Next to the meadow, there was a dark forest.

And in the middle of the forest, there lived a hungry wolf.

4

"Peter, you must stay in the garden," said Grandfather. "You must never go into the meadow on your own."

"But why?" said Peter.

"Because there is a hungry wolf in the forest. He might come out of the forest and eat you up!" said Grandfather.

Peter looked over the garden wall. The meadow looked very beautiful.

A little red bird flew up to a tree.

"Hello, Peter!" called the bird. "Why don't you come into the meadow?"

So Peter climbed over the garden wall and went into the meadow.

There was a pond in the middle of the green meadow.

A duck waddled past Peter, jumped into the pond and swam away.

The little red bird flew down to the duck.

"Come back!" she said. "What a funny walk you have! Why don't you fly like me?"

"I don't want to fly like you," said the duck. "Why don't you swim like me?"

The two birds were very cross with each other, and they made a lot of noise.

Suddenly, Peter saw a cat crawling towards the birds.

"Look out!" called Peter. "The cat will get you!"

15

At once, the little red bird flew up to the top of the tree and the duck swam to the middle of the pond.

The cat saw that she would have to wait a little longer to eat.

She walked over to the tree.

Just then, Peter's grandfather came into the garden.

He looked over the wall and saw Peter in the meadow.

He was very cross with Peter.

"Come back at once. I told you not to go into the meadow," said Grandfather.

So Peter climbed over the wall and went back into the garden with his grandfather.

Suddenly, the wolf came out of the forest.

He saw the little red bird, the duck and the cat. He was so hungry, that he wanted to eat them all.

23

The cat climbed to the very top of the tree, where the little red bird was sitting.

The two of them waited to see what might happen.

The duck jumped out of the pond and ran and ran. She ran as fast as she could, but the hungry wolf ran faster. He caught her in his mouth. Then he ate her up.

Then the wolf walked round and round the tree where the cat and the little red bird were sitting.

The hungry wolf looked up at them.

The cat and the bird were very frightened.

Peter found a very long rope.
Then he climbed on top of the
garden wall.

"Fly around the wolf's head!" he
called to the little red bird. "Make
him dizzy! But keep away from
his mouth!"

The little red bird flew round and round the wolf's head.

The hungry wolf tried to catch the little red bird, but after a time, he was very dizzy.

Peter climbed up the big tree. Then he let down the rope and caught the wolf by the tail.

The wolf jumped up and down and tried to get away.

But Peter held onto the rope.

"You won't get away from me!" he said.

Just then, Grandfather came out of the garden and saw Peter sitting in the tree.

"What are you doing up there?" he called.

"I've caught the wolf," said Peter. "Look!"

Suddenly, some hunters came into the meadow.

They were looking for the wolf.

"Here he is," said Peter. "Please will you take him away, so that I can play in the meadow."

So the hunters took the wolf to another forest – a long way away from Peter and his grandfather, the cat, and the little red bird.

They never saw him again.

41

And Peter's grandfather let him
play in the beautiful meadow,
with the little red bird and the cat.

Read It Yourself is a series of graded readers designed to give young children a confident and successful start to reading.

Level 4 is suitable for children who are ready to read longer stories with a wider vocabulary. The stories are told in a simple way and with a richness of language which makes reading a rewarding experience. Repetition of new vocabulary reinforces the words the child is learning and exciting illustrations bring the action to life.

About this book

At this stage children may prefer to read the story aloud to an adult without first discussing the pictures. Although children are now progressing towards silent, independent reading, they need to know that adult help and encouragement is readily available. When children meet a word they do not know, these words can be worked out by looking at the beginning letter (*what sound does this letter make?*) and other sounds the child recognises within the word. The child can then decide which word makes sense.

Nearly independent readers need lots of praise and encouragement.